No Groundhog Day for NoNo

Written by Cindy Taylor
Illustrated by Mary Travis

To Stevie, Ruben, Augie, and River: my heart 🖤
- CLT

To Jack and Annie: I love you as big as the sun ☀
- MKT

To Phil's Faithful Followers:

None of the events in this book are true.
No one - not even by mistake or mishap -
would ever take the place of
Punxsutawney Phil.

NoNo was Punxsutawney Phil's distant cousin.

He lived with his best friend and Phil's handler,
Rainmaker.

Rainmaker took good care of NoNo, feeding him his
favorite banana and carrot treat every day.

NoNo was in awe of his big cousin, Phil, and yearned to be like him. In fact, NoNo wanted to BE Phil!

Rainmaker explained to NoNo that Phil had been Punxsutawney's weather prognosticator since 1887, and no one would ever take his place. Rainmaker told NoNo, "No, no, no, NoNo, just no. It won't work. Look for a different job."

February 2nd rolled around, and Rainmaker would not allow this jealous cousin to even attend Groundhog Day.

He said, "No, no, no, NoNo. Just no!"

NoNo disagreed.

So when Rainmaker left for his duties
at Gobbler's Knob, NoNo jumped on
the hood of a passing blue bug and
hitched a ride to the big event.

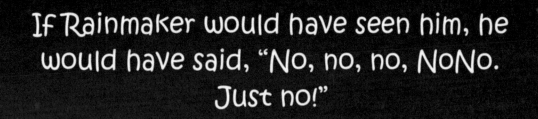

If Rainmaker would have seen him, he would have said, "No, no, no, NoNo. Just no!"

But he didn't see.

GOBBLER'S KNOB

Upon arrival at the knob, this crazy varmint jumped off the car, zigzagged and ran through the crowd of Phil's faithful followers and jumped right on stage.

Rainmaker's eyes got VERY BIG upon seeing this. He yelled, "No, no, no, NoNo! Just no!"

Too late. NoNo turned to face the crowd. Now it was HIS eyes that got big. Nono was center stage, in the middle of top-hat-wearing men, in front of forty thousand people, with the TV cameras and bright lights starting to focus on him.

NoNo's two little teeth chattered as he mumbled, "No, no, no!" He had to find a way out NOW!

"No, no, no!"

It just so happened that the Groundhog Club
President had already knocked three times on Phil's
door so it was beginning to open. Phil was crawling
out to make his weather prediction to the world.
But all NoNo saw was his escape! Jumping into
action, he dove through the open crack. Realizing
the bad collision that was about to happen,
Rainmaker shouted, "No, no, no, NoNo! Just no!"

Too late. Phil was barreled over and pushed
back, deep into his burrow.

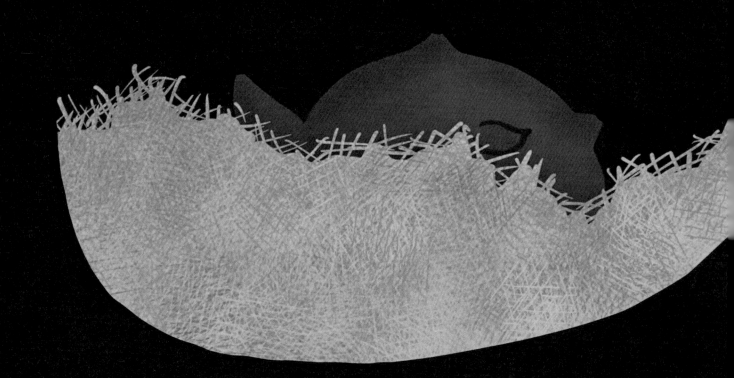

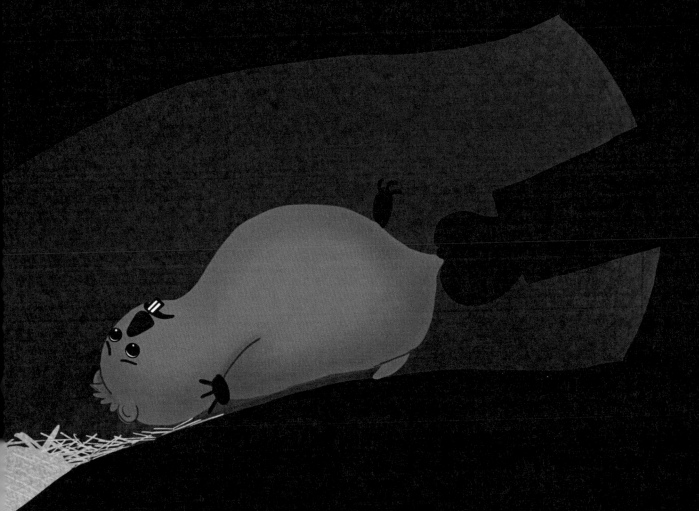

Not knowing what else to do, and running out
of precious time, Rainmaker grabbed the
closest groundhog he could. Big whistling
words echoed from the back of the burrow,
"No, no, no, Rainmaker! Just No!"

Too late.
With a grin as
wide as the
shadow he was
now looking at,
NoNo was held
high in the air! His
dream had come
true.

Now through his two little front teeth, NoNo muttered to the Rainmaker, " Yes, yes, yes, Rainmaker, just YES!"
And no one ever knew.

The end.

Made in United States
North Haven, CT
16 November 2021